Jammie Day!

SWISH

For Cliffy, of course—C.S.

For Penny, and her little polka dot pajamas—B.K.

Text © 2017 Carrie Snyder
Illustrations © 2017 Brooke Kerrigan

Owlkids Books acknowledges the financial support of the Canada Council for the Arts, the Ontario Arts Council, the Government of Canada through the Canada Book Fund (CBF) and the Government of Ontario through the Ontario Media Development Corporation's Book Initiative for our publishing activities.

Published in Canada by
Owlkids Books Inc.
10 Lower Spadina Avenue
Toronto, ON M5V 2Z2

Published in the United States by
Owlkids Books Inc.
1700 Fourth Street
Berkeley, CA 94710

Library and Archives Canada Cataloguing in Publication

Snyder, Carrie, author
    Jammie day! / written by Carrie Snyder ; illustrated by Brooke Kerrigan.

ISBN 978-1-77147-200-5 (hardcover)

    I. Kerrigan, Brooke, illustrator II. Title.

PS8587.N785J34 2017   jC813'.6   C2017-900002-0
Library of Congress Control Number: 2016962526

Edited by: Debbie Rogosin
Designed by: Barb Kelly

ONTARIO ARTS COUNCIL
CONSEIL DES ARTS DE L'ONTARIO
an Ontario government agency
un organisme du gouvernement de l'Ontario

Canada Council   Conseil des Arts
for the Arts   du Canada

Canadä

Manufactured in Shenzhen, Guangdong, China, in April 2017, by WKT Co. Ltd.
Job #16B3152

A   B   C   D   E   F

Publisher of Chirp, chickaDEE and OWL | Owlkids Books is a division of
www.owlkidsbooks.com

Bayard
CANADA

Jammie Day!

By Carrie Snyder
Illustrated by Brooke Kerrigan

meow

Owlkids Books

Cliffy was in the middle.
He had a big brother and
a big sister. He had a little
brother and a little sister.
He had a nice cat that never
scratched him, not even
when Cliffy petted her fur
the wrong way.

Cliffy's big brother and big sister thought they knew everything.

Cliffy's little brother and little sister hardly knew anything!

Cliffy was in the middle. He
knew what he knew. But most
of all, he knew what he liked.

One morning, Cliffy woke up, went
downstairs, and got breakfast. Nobody noticed.
He turned his porridge into a volcano and let
the cat eat from his spoon. Nobody noticed.
It was getting late. Finally, somebody noticed.
"Cliffy!" said his mom. "Get dressed! It's time
for school!"

But Cliffy did not want to get dressed.
So he did something a little bit funny.
A little bit *fuzzy*.
   "It's Jammie Day," said Cliffy.
   "Oh?" said his mom. She might not have
been paying attention.

Cliffy put on his boots and his coat over top of his pajamas. Then he put on his scarf and his hat, and he walked to school.

"Are you wearing pajamas?"
asked Cliffy's teacher.
"It's Jammie Day," said Cliffy.
"Oh?" said his teacher. She might
not have been paying attention.

The only tricky part about
Jammie Day was the zipper.

The best part about
Jammie Day was the
cozy flannel.

No, the best part about Jammie Day
was being super-duper comfy.

No, wait, the *best*
part was the footies!

SWISH

"Cool pajamas," said all the girls in Cliffy's class.
"Awesome pajamas," said all the boys in Cliffy's class.

"Thanks," said Cliffy. He didn't tell them it was
Jammie Day. The kids knew. They were paying attention.

After school, Cliffy's dad gave
him a snack. He asked, "What are
you wearing?"

"It's Jammie Day," said Cliffy.

"Oh?" said his dad. He might not
have been paying attention.

The next morning, Cliffy woke up, went downstairs, and got breakfast.

"Get dressed! You're late!" said his mom.

But Cliffy knew what he knew, and he knew what he liked.

"It's Jammie Day," said Cliffy.

"Oh?" said his mom. "Again?"

"It's Jammie Day!" said Cliffy. To his teacher.

"Oh?" said his teacher. "Again?"

"It's Jammie Day!" said Cliffy. To the girls and boys in his class.

"Oh," said the boys and girls. "We know!" Half of them were wearing pajamas, too.

"It's Jammie Week!" said Cliffy.

To his mom.

To his dad.

To his brothers and sisters.

To the cat.

"It's Jammie Month!" said Cliffy.
To anyone who would pay attention.

Cliffy was in the middle. And that's the best place to be if you know what you know and you know what you like.
"Jammie Year!"

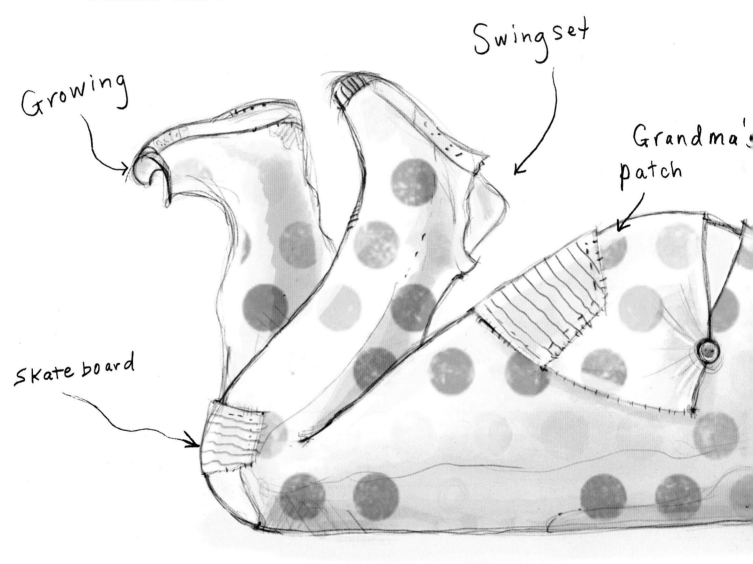

Growing

Swingset

Grandma's patch

Skateboard

mud
fight

Grape Juice

potato sack
race

31901061104875